# LIT [illegible] DROPS OF JOY



MAHENDRA VIKRAM SHAH

ISBN 978-1-68586-957-1

This book is dedicated to my family members and my special friend because of him, you will be reading it today.

# Contents

# Acknowledgements

I would like to thank my family and friends for their continuous support.

But special thanks to a special friend because of whom I was motivated to write and publish my book . Merci beaucoup for coming into my life.

CHAPTER ONE

# Liitle drops of joy

Kshitiz walking towards the mid of the river with knife and his hand full of blood.

"Loving in a wrong way makes us sad
Loving a wrong person makes us cry
Begging infront of wrong person brings tears in our eyes
Smooth path makes us useless
One day suddenly we keep our foot on the thorns
Because we don't know how and when to stop
And we don't want to look back"
Eyes are full of dryness
Heart is empty but seems full ' an illusion'
We look into the sky and think now it's an end
Moving towards wrong destiny makes us sad
Doors are closed but not our believes
When we broke down we are left alone
Not able to forget our sorrows neither heal them up"

Shrey and Kshitiz taking care of each other in school, growing together as best friends. They started sharing a bond which is beyond friendship may be that's love for each other . Spending hours together .They don't care about day and night. They don't care about their social life. For them only Shrey and Kshitiz is the world.

FIVE YEARS LATER

Bougainvillea High School is full of noise as it's a day for Parent's Teacher Meet. Crowd and crowd everywhere in the school not a place to step. A young beautiful mentor 'Aastha' , busy with the parents briefing them about their childs performance and explaining them about the newly introduced curriculum.

Lokesh , A young man of 30 enters her classroom with his nephew to discuss about his academic performance. Aastha offered him a seat . They both greet each other. Aastha shares that young kid is very intelligent but on the other hand he is naughty too. Both of them discussed about child performance and she appreciates the young kid for always being active in the class. In between Lokesh even tries to flirt with her where she find its going to the wrong direction now. So she finishes up the meet and Lokesh leaves from the school.

Kshitiz doing office work on his laptop and suddenly Shrey comes to hold him from behind. Kshitiz turns back says "Oh Why you wake up so early dear ? You would have slept more as you came late from the office yesterday." Shrey replied "Just wanted to see you that what you hiding from me' .

'Oh man is anything hidden between us' replied Kshitiz . Shrey touches his cheeks and kiss him ' it's just a joke baby'.

Kshitiz opens his notepad and started writing the poem. As he loves writing. Kshitiz wrote the title 'Love is everything ' suddenly Shrey pokes him by saying 'Oh ! What a nonsense . Make it Love is just an illusion. Khsitiz gets angry they both started fighting.

Lokesh teasing his nephew that he has become very naughty need to complain his mom and dad. On contrary his nephew started teasing him about Aastha. He noticed that how his uncle was flirting with him. Later Lokesh demand his nephew to do his secret work next morning.

Shrey with his mother in the temple , they leave the premises while gossiping. Shrey Mother , Mrs. Roy says ' Dear son you have damn busy life why do you take me to the temple everyday. I will come of my own from tomorrow. Shrey justifies to his mom that it's nothing like that he love spending time with her from this hectic schedule.

Shrey to his mom 'I have you won't mind mom that we will in the same city still not together it's not because of my office but I am looking for the nearby job'.

Mom replies 'No child ! After your dad left us you are only one who is taking care of the home financially. So just focus on your job. Don't think about it'

Shrey 'But I don't feel safe for you as you are alone here. Why don't you shift with me ? '

'Don't worry child someone should be there to look after the house and Everyday Aastha comes to meet me after her school .So I don't feel lonely' replied Mrs. Roy.

'See that kid Mom ! How cute and naughty he is. Was I the same when I was this small' asked Shrey.

'Yes you were but I am happy that I got such a lovely son who cares for me a lot' replied Mrs. Roy.

Chirping of birds and beautiful sunrise , a day began at Bougainvillea High School. Kunal , Lokesh's nephew handing over the rose to Aastha on behalf of Lokesh. Aastha accepted it silently to maintain the decorum of the classroom. At the end of the school she returns back the rose to Kunal asked him to give back to his uncle as she has allergy from the rose.

Kshitiz and Shrey sitting in a peaceful area near to river.

Kshitiz 'Shrey there is a party at my friend's place I want you to come along with me' . Shrey replies 'No, not interested in your social media friends'.

Kshitiz says 'All my friends come along with their partners but I am the only one who always go alone , when I talk about you to them they tease me by saying that you are imaginary.

Birds chirping outside , Kshitiz wakes up and remove the curtain , goes to bed again. He wakes up Shrey . 'I don't think you love me anymore the way you reacted last night. I think we shoul think about our relatoionship' whispers Kshitiz.

'Why don't you understand . It is not acceptable in the society. I am the only child of my mother who need to fulfill all her dreams and desire. She has started looking for a girl for me and I can't disappoint her. Please understand' Shrey replied.

After listening to this Kshitiz wakes up , went for the shower in the anger.... Shrey tries to convince him.

'I gave you my everything thing and now why you doing this to me ? How can you marry a girl ? when you say I am your everything' Kshitiz asked.

'Don't worry baby , we will be in relationship and I will be loving you in the same way even after my marriage' replied Shrey.

'Don't be selfish Shrey, you don't any right to destroy anyone's life like. How can you even think of doing it ? Why don't you talk to your mother about it. She is so understanding she will understand. Even I share about you with my parent' asked Kshitiz.

'Are you crazy ??? Don't you dare to think of it.... Whatever bond we have it will be just inside a room for the world we are only the friends' replied Shrey

Shrey leaves and bangs the door forcefully.

Khsitiz screaming from behind don't leave me alone , I need you .

Shrey at his home taking shower comes out in a towel . Look at his bare body, full of tears in his eyes. Mrs. Roy called him up for breakfast.

Mrs. Roy serves the breakfast to him.

'Mom , I have to go office early. I will have my breakfast there only' Shrey to Mrs. Roy.

'Ok , Just take the juice. I have to ask you something if you have sometime' asked Mrs. Roy

Yes Mom ! Please say..........

'Beta, Now you are in mid 30's and I think this is the suitable age for you. I have selected Aastha for you, according to me she is perfect for you Anyways its your life you have decide. As you also know beta you are in the growing age and you need someone to take care of you. Do think about it and let me kow....' says Mrs. Roy

'I know Mom , whatever you will decide will be better for me.... But still I will think and revert you back' replied Shrey.

Shrey in his cabin, not able to work properly , only thinking about his mom and Kshitiz, He suffered from the severe headache, He asked his assistant to get the medicine.

It's a departure time in School, Buses and students leaving the campus. Lokesh in bike waiting for Aastha to come out. After waiting for about 30 minutes he saw Aastha coming along with her colleague.

'oh god ! This Kunal's uncle again........ I m fed up of him. Just see the way he is staring at me' Aastha to colleague.

'Anyways he is smart hunk' replied her colleague.

'Shut up ! you know yesterday he send the rose for me... I don't know he want to create this trouble yar' says Aastha.

Lokesh keep on staring at her with the decent smile. Aastha starts her car started moving..... Lokesh followed her ...after a long game . Aastha got melted and She throws the smile of friendship.

Shrey knocks the door.... Khsitiz opens and Shrey standing infront with bouquet and gift. Bending on his knees and apologizing ‘ I am sorry sweetheart’.

Khsitiz in the rude tone ‘if you think with this gift I will be convinced, then you are wrong .... Please leave me alone’

Khsitiz took his bouquet and throw it on the table. Closes the half door on Shrey’s face. Shrey hold the door and enters inside.

‘Can’t we think of it later.... Don’t do this to me Kshitiz . I can’t live without you. I love you so much my dear’ says Shrey.

‘Love ???? Do you even know the exact meaning of love.... You would have not left me alone in the morning when I needed you’ replied Kshitiz

‘I am extremely sorry dear . I will never leave you alone . I promise’ said Shrey

They hug and kiss each other.

‘And I promise, I will soon share about our relationship to my mom’ added Shrey.

It was an noisy classroom , Aastha enters the class and asked students to maintain decorum. Lokesh nephew visited her with a piece of paper ‘SEE YOU AT 4 PM @PINE HUT CAFÉ’.

There is a knock on Khistiz’s door, Shrey opens the door found Mrs. Jain, Khsitiz’s Mother standing in anger. He greets her with a smile. On contrary she gave a rude look to him.

The clock strike at 4PM , Lokesh waiting at Pine Hut Café. He saw Aastha coming in a beautiful dress. They greet each other and he pulled the chair for her.

Mrs. Jain sits on the sofa full of anger. He asked Shrey, where is Kshitiz ? Shrey replied that he has gone to the market. Mrs. Jain is not able to control and she warned Shrey to stay away from her son. Kshitiz enters and listens to their conversation but he ignores. He tries to hug her mother but she refused to do that.

'What happen Maa ? Why you being so rude ?' asked Shrey

'What happen ? As if you don't know.... Me and your father have good reputation in the society and now because of you, it will dig in honor .' said Mrs. Jain

Shrey and kshitiz try to convince Mrs. Jain but she is so furious that she is not ready to listen to anyone. Instead she started misbehaving with Shrey.

'I don't know why this man has done your mind wash..... that you are not ready to listen to your parent' says Mrs. Jain.

'Please Mom, Don't say anything to him ........ he love me like anything' replied Kshitiz

'Love .... My foot, You people even know what is love ?.... He is gay and they are only known for Sex....... They can use anyone for their lust... Whenever his desires will be over... you will be left alone' says Mrs. Jain.

Kshitiz screamed 'Control your tongue Mom ! Just think before you say... I am your child and I am also gay ...... I am proud of being gay..... That's true'

Mrs. Jain Slaps Kshitiz... Don't you ever dare to speak in such tone with me.

Mrs. Jain totally feels broken and she leaves the house.

It's was the pleasant evening, Shrey's Mother serves the dinner on the table.

'Oh Mom ! I am too hungry.... What's for the dinner today ?' Shrey asked.

'Today Aastha cooked for your favorite meal Palak Panner and Mixed Vegetables' Mom replied.

She added ' I have shared my decision with Aastha about you both. As you know she respects me a lot she couldn't say no to me. Now its your both decision ... I will be waiting.'

Aastha comes out from the kitchen , Shrey and Aastha greet each other with the pleasant smile. Three of them enjoy the meal together by talking about each other. Shrey appreciated the food made by Aastha. Suddenly Mrs. Roy talked about their wedding .... Both blushed and nodded with the smile. Shrey leaves for Kshitiz house after having dinner.

Kshitiz wakes up in the mid night up, found that Shrey is not beside . He moves out of the bed ...... Shrey is seems tensed continuously looking outside the window. Kshitiz hugs him from front and apologizes about his mother's behavior but there is no response he seems still.

'If you want to keep our relationship secret , I am ready for that... but please say something' Kshitiz added.

Shrey kisses him and replied 'It's just office work load nothing that... just go to bed we have to wake up early for work'.

Clock strike at 4PM , It's crowdy evening in Pine Hut Café . Clouds are getting grey.... Seems some big storms is about to come.

'What ?? How can you this ? We love each other Aastha.... You things it's a puppet show... why can't you NO to them... we love eachother..' Lokesh furiously shouted.

'I am sorry Lokesh. After my parent left this world Mrs. Roy is the only one who supported in every step. She is like my mother. She has done a lot for me.' Aastha replied.

'Will you be happy with Shrey ? you love me right. Think about us.... Please don't do this to me dear' Lokesh said furiously.

'I am sorry Lokesh, please forget the moments that we spent together as I can't say NO' Aastha replied.

Aastha gets up from the chair with heavy heart and full of tears .... She leaves.

Shrey and kshitiz in the kitchen cooking for each other , listening the music and dancing together... Suddenly Shrey got a call from his mother... She asked him to come urgently.

As soon as Shrey reached his house , he found 5 cars which is fimilar to him is parked outside his gate. He is surprised to see his Maternal and Paternal Uncles and their families. It's seemed that they all have been gathered here for some occasion , Yes his guess was right its sudden planned engagement of his with Aastha. Shrey is blanked ... His cousin took him to his room to make him ready for the event.

As five hours have been passed .... Kshitiz continuously tries to call Shrey but he don't get any response.. He is worried . He could not wait anymore . He began to ride his bike towards Shrey's home.

Engagement function begans at their home... Shrey is out with the fake smile and blank mind as its all of sudden. Aastha arriving in the beautiful attire but full of heavy heart from inside. As soon as ring ceremony began... Kshitiz arrived , He saw from outside now he is fully broken .... He rana away from the place.

Kshitiz arrived his house , where he throw all the stuffs and damaged the house badly. On the other side Aastha and Shrey are in the same situation but with heavy heart they are ready to compromise.

Next morning Kshitiz came outside Shrey outside called his maid and asked her to hand over the piece of paper to Shrey. Maid handed it to Mrs. Roy as Shrey has left for the office.

It's 6 PM of the evening , Shrey is back from work ... He found that his mother is full of tears and she could not ate anything since morning. She handed over the letter to Shrey and asked him to read it loud.

Dear Shrey,

Yesterday , when I saw you and Aastha together , I missed those moments that we have spent together. The time we spent together , the way you loved me and cared for me but when I saw you together I think it's the end of our journey now. I just want to drown in the memories and the moments that we have spent together.

Now I am going away from you where no one could find me and I will be in peace with full of our memories. I don't want you and your fake love now. Never blame yourself for this. I know you want to keep your mom happy. I wish you also be happy with Aastha.

Just promise me , never think about me , never ever be in relationship with a boy as it might heart your family. Good bye Shrey.

only yours,

Kshitiz

Shrey started apologizing his mom for this , on contrary Mrs. Roy apologizes Shrey that she could not understand her son and his desire. She added 'How can I be happy Shrey ? If you are broken from inside.' She started crying and apologizing him. She asked to go look for Kshitiz.

Shrey reaches Kshitiz's house everything is broken and damaged ... No one is there. He ran towards their favorite place . where he found Khsitiz already lying beside the river with full of blood strains.... Shrey holds him in his arms and promised I will never ever leave you.